First published by Parragon in 2012
Parragon
Queen Street House
4 Queen Street
Bath BA1 1HE, UK
www.parragon.com

Editor: Lindsay Kaubi; Designer: Jim Willmott
Production controller: Emma Fulleylove

ISBN 978-1-4454-6503-6

Printed in China

Disney

Bambi

Bath · New York · Singapore · Hong Kong · Cologne · Delhi
Melbourne · Amsterdam · Johannesburg · Auckland · Shenzhen

One spring morning, there was great excitement in the forest. A new Prince had been born. His name was Bambi. He was the son of a noble stag, the Great Prince of the Forest.

Bambi lay asleep by his mother's side. When he woke, the little spotted fawn saw happy smiling faces all around him.

"My name's Thumper," said a friendly rabbit. Bambi smiled.

It wasn't long before Bambi was ready to explore the forest. He made lots of new friends.

"The forest is a wonderful place!" Bambi thought to himself.

One day, Bambi and Thumper were playing. Birds fluttered above their heads. Thumper pointed at one and said, "That's a bird."

Bambi repeated the word, "Bird!"

Then a butterfly fluttered by. Bambi called out, "Bird!"

"No," giggled Thumper, "that's a butterfly."

Bambi turned to a patch of brightly colored flowers and shouted, "Butterfly!"

Thumper laughed. "No," he cried, "that's a flower!"

Bambi bent down to smell a patch of brightly colored flowers. Suddenly, a small black and white head popped up from under the petals.

"Flower!" said Bambi, again.

Thumper rolled on the ground with laughter. "That's not a flower, that's a skunk!" he said.

"He can call me Flower if he wants to," said the little skunk.

Bambi had made another new friend.

The days passed happily for Bambi. One morning his mother took him to a new place—the meadow.

The meadow was wide and open. Bambi's mother warned him that they had to be very careful. "There are no trees here to hide us," she said.

Bambi ran off to play. Soon, he found a pond. He leaned over and looked into the water at his own reflection. Suddenly, another reflection appeared. It belonged to a female fawn about the same age as Bambi. She wanted to play.

Bambi felt very shy. He ran back to his mother and tried to hide.

"It's all right," Bambi's mother said. "That's Faline. She just wants to be your friend. Go and say hello."

Bambi went back to Faline. When she began to chase him, Bambi chased her. Soon, the two fawns were playing hide-and-seek in the tall grass.

Out in the meadow a group of stags came galloping by. Then another stag—the biggest one of all—stopped and looked straight at Bambi. It was Bambi's father, the Great Prince of the Forest. He had come to warn the deer that there was danger nearby.

As the deer dashed toward the trees, Bambi couldn't find his mother. He began to panic. The next moment his father was beside him.

Bambi followed the Great Prince into the forest and was overjoyed to see his mother there too.

Later that day, Bambi asked his mother what the danger had been.

"Man was in the Forest," she told him.

The Great
Prince of the
Forest.

Time passed swiftly, summer and autumn passed, and the weather grew colder.

One morning, Bambi woke up to find the wind had turned cold and the whole world was covered in a soft white blanket. Bambi's mother saw his surprise.

"That's snow," she said. "It means winter has come."

Bambi was having great fun making hoof prints in the snow, when he heard Thumper calling him.

"...winter has come."

"Come on, you can slide too!"

Bambi found his friend sliding across an icy pond.

"The water's stiff," called Thumper. "Come on, you can slide too!"

Bambi rushed over to join him. But he fell on his tummy with a loud—THUD!

Thumper tried to teach Bambi how to skate, pushing his back legs up, then pulling his front legs straight. But they both ended up in a heap, skidding and sliding across the glittering ice.

Winter was fun at first, but after a while, Bambi longed for the warm spring days that had brought with them delicious grass and flowers. As time passed by, there was less and less food and all the animals grew hungry. Eventually, there was nothing for Bambi and his mother to eat except the bark on the trees.

One day, when it felt a little warmer, Bambi and his mother went to the meadow to search for food. There they found a small patch of green grass peeping out of the snow.

Bambi and his mother ate the grass hungrily.

Suddenly, Bambi's mother looked up and sniffed the air. She sensed danger.

"Go back to the forest!" she ordered Bambi. "Quickly! Run!"

Bambi raced across the meadow with his mother behind him. There was a loud—BANG!

"Faster, Bambi, and don't look back!" his mother shouted.

Bambi ran and ran, his heart pounding as his hooves kicked up snow behind him.

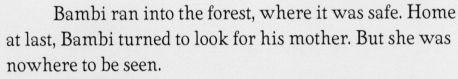

Bambi ran into the forest, where it was safe. Home at last, Bambi turned to look for his mother. But she was nowhere to be seen.

Bambi's heart thumped with panic. He called for his mother again and again. The little fawn began to cry.

Just then, his father appeared by his side.

"Your mother cannot be with you any longer," he told Bambi gently.

Bambi lowered his head sadly, and swallowed back his tears.

"Come, my son," the stag told him.

The Great Prince would now protect his son until he could look after himself.

The little fawn
began to cry.

"Flower's
twitterpated!"

Time flew by quickly, and the long winter was at last over. Spring brought with it many changes. Bambi was now a handsome young buck with antlers, Thumper was a large rabbit, and Flower a fully grown skunk.

One day, Flower met a female skunk and fell in love.

"Oh, no!" said Thumper. "Flower's twitterpated! Owl says it happens to everyone in the springtime!"

"It won't happen to me," Bambi said.

"Me neither," Thumper agreed.

Minutes later, Thumper met a female rabbit, and he too was twitterpated.

Bambi wandered off for a drink.

Bambi still didn't quite understand what twitterpated was until he saw a familiar reflection in the water as he was drinking from the pond.

"Hello, Bambi!" said a sweet female voice. "Don't you remember me? I'm Faline." The doe giggled and licked his face.

Bambi suddenly felt dizzy, as if he were light as a feather. This, he thought, must be what twitterpated means!

Bambi fought fiercely....

But someone else liked Faline, too. A young stag appeared, and he tried to take her away from Bambi.

The two deer locked antlers, tossing each other against the hard ground. Bambi fought fiercely, pushing the stag to the edge of a cliff. Then he butted the stag with all his might, sending him rolling down into the river below. The stag limped off into the forest, leaving Bambi and Faline alone.

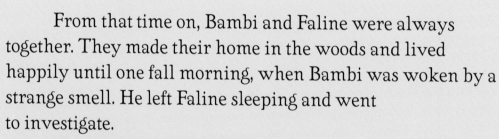

From that time on, Bambi and Faline were always together. They made their home in the woods and lived happily until one fall morning, when Bambi was woken by a strange smell. He left Faline sleeping and went to investigate.

He climbed a cliff and saw smoke in the distance. Just then, his father came up beside him.

"Man has returned," he said. "We must go deep into the forest—quickly!"

Bambi rushed to warn Faline.

"Man has returned...."

Fear spread among the animals as the men
drew nearer.

"Bambi, Bambi!" Faline cried in terror. She could hear
the sounds of angry dogs close by. She scrambled up a steep
slope just as a pack of snarling hounds burst out of the bushes
behind her. Barking and biting, they chased her up a rocky
cliff, snapping at her heels—she was trapped!

Just then, the dogs turned to attack something else.
Bambi was fighting them off so that Faline could run away.
Bambi rushed at the dogs, and Faline bounded up the cliff
to safety.

Bambi fought off the pack of dogs and turned to follow
Faline. Suddenly, he heard a loud—BANG!

He felt a terrible pain and fell to the ground.

The forest
was on fire....

Bambi raised his head weakly to see smoke pouring
through the trees and animals running in fear. Flames from man's
campfire swept toward the deer. The forest was on fire, but Bambi
could not move.

Once more his father appeared at his side. "You must get up!"
said the Great Prince.

The young Prince staggered to his feet and followed his father through the burning forest. Smoke filled the air, and red flames spread over the trees and bushes, surrounding the once beautiful forest in an eerie orange glow.

"Follow me," the Great Prince said. "We'll be safe in the river."

They came to a waterfall and jumped. Down and down they fell and crashed into the water far below, just as a flaming tree crashed inches behind them.

Bambi and his father waded through the water and headed toward an island in the middle of the river.

Many other birds and animals had already found shelter on the island. Faline was there too. She was overjoyed to see Bambi again and gently licked his wounded shoulder.

They watched that night as fire destroyed their forest home—all the towering trees and delicate blossoms were now blackened. But tomorrow, they knew, when the fire was out and Man was gone, the animals would bravely rebuild their homes.

When the fire finally burned out, the animals returned to the forest.

After a long, hard winter, spring arrived. New grass and flowers grew where the fire had been. The forest was beautiful once again.

One warm morning, all the animals and birds came to see Faline and her two new fawns. Standing nearby was their proud father, Bambi, the new Great Prince of the Forest.

Faline and her
two new fawns.